D0892515

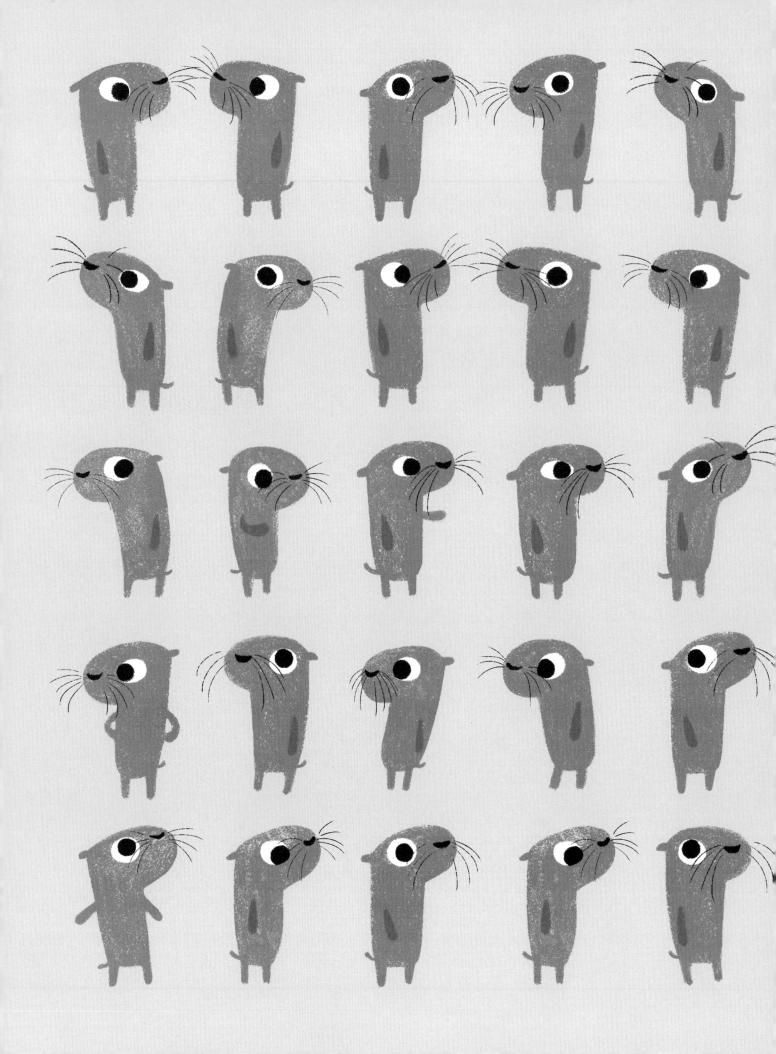

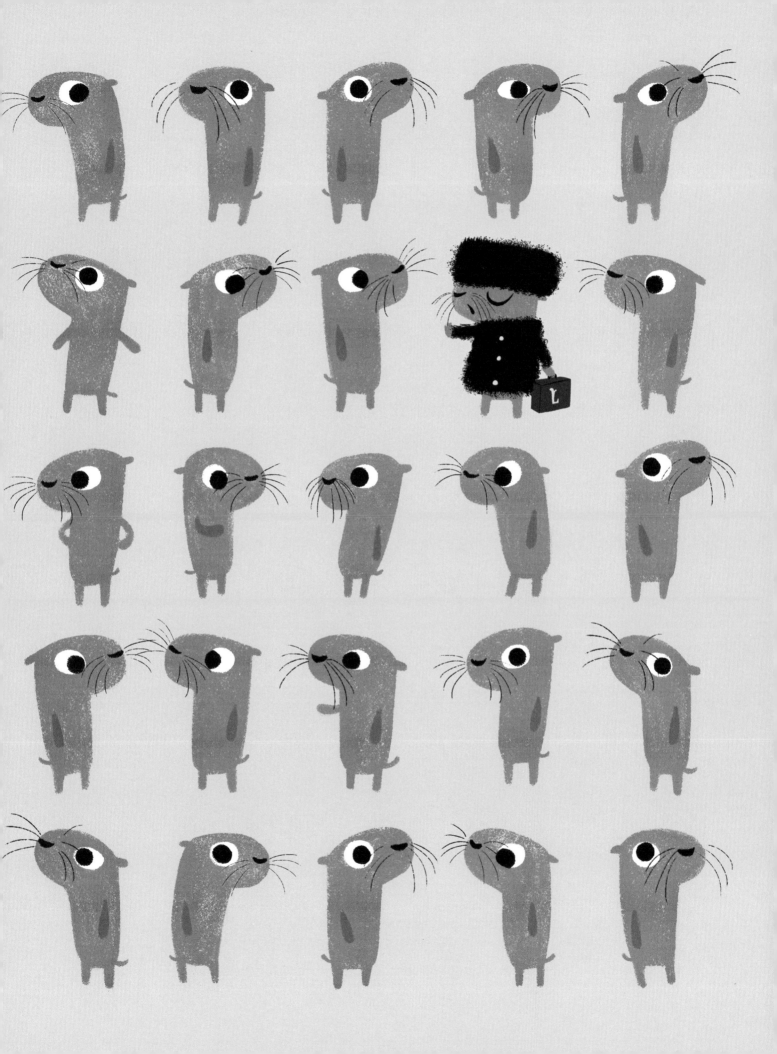

To Johnny K, Hailey, and Josephine. — J. B.

For Leo. — N. S.

Originally published in the United States in 2016 under the title *Leaping Lemmings!* by Sterling Publishing Co., Inc.

First published in the United Kingdom in 2017
by Pavilion Children's Books, 43 Great Ormond St, London WC1N 3HZ

Text © 2016 by John Briggs
Illustrations © 2016 by Nicola Slater

ISBN 978-1-84365-338-7

Printed and bound by RR Donnelley – Asia Printing Solutions Ltd.

10 9 8 7 6 5 4 3 2 1

This book can be ordered directly from the publisher online
at www.pavilionbooks.com, or try your local bookshop.

The artwork for this book was created digitally.

DON'T LEAP, LARRY!

by
JOHN BRIGGS

illustrated by
NICOLA SLATER

PAVILION

Can you tell these two lemmings apart?

No?

That's because all lemmings look alike,
sound alike, and act alike.

Except one lemming . . .

When all the other lemmings dug tunnels to keep warm, he went sledging with the puffins.

When the other lemmings
squeaked and squealed, he
banged on the bongos he got
from the seals.

When the other lemmings ate moss from under
a rock, he ordered pepperoni pizza with extra
cheese and hot sauce.

Yes, this lemming was an oddball.
He stood out in every lemming photo.

Norway trip

And he was easy to spot at hide-and-seek.

The other lemmings tried to talk with him.

"He wants to be called Larry."

"I'm not calling him Larry."

"What's a Larry?"

"No lemming's ever been called Larry."

"No lemming's ever been called anything."

"I hear he wants to be called Mary."

**The lemmings called a big meeting,
and they only had one question:**

Larry knew he didn't fit in, so he tried something
else no other lemming had ever done.

He went to live with the seals.

He moved in with the puffins.

You live on CLIFFS?!

He visited the polar bears.

Larry ran all the way home to the lemmings,
who were also running – straight for the cliff!

Larry raced in front of his friends as fast as he could. He made a sharp U-turn . . . and the lemmings followed him!

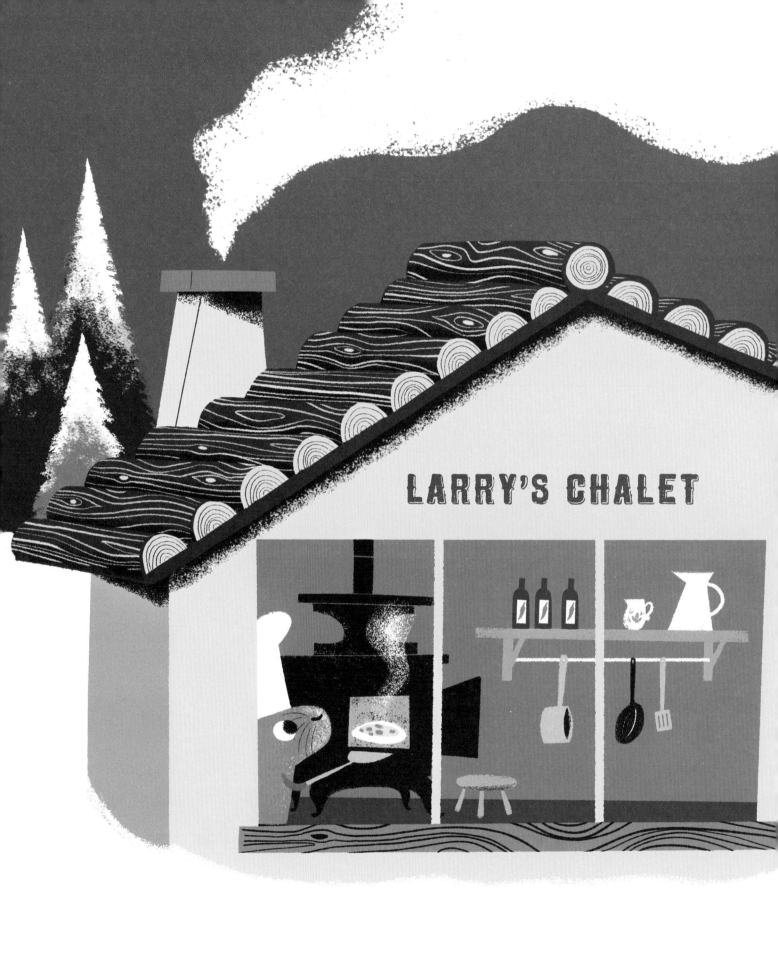

And the lemmings didn't stop following Larry until every last one was safe at home enjoying a hero's feast of pepperoni pizza with extra cheese and hot sauce.

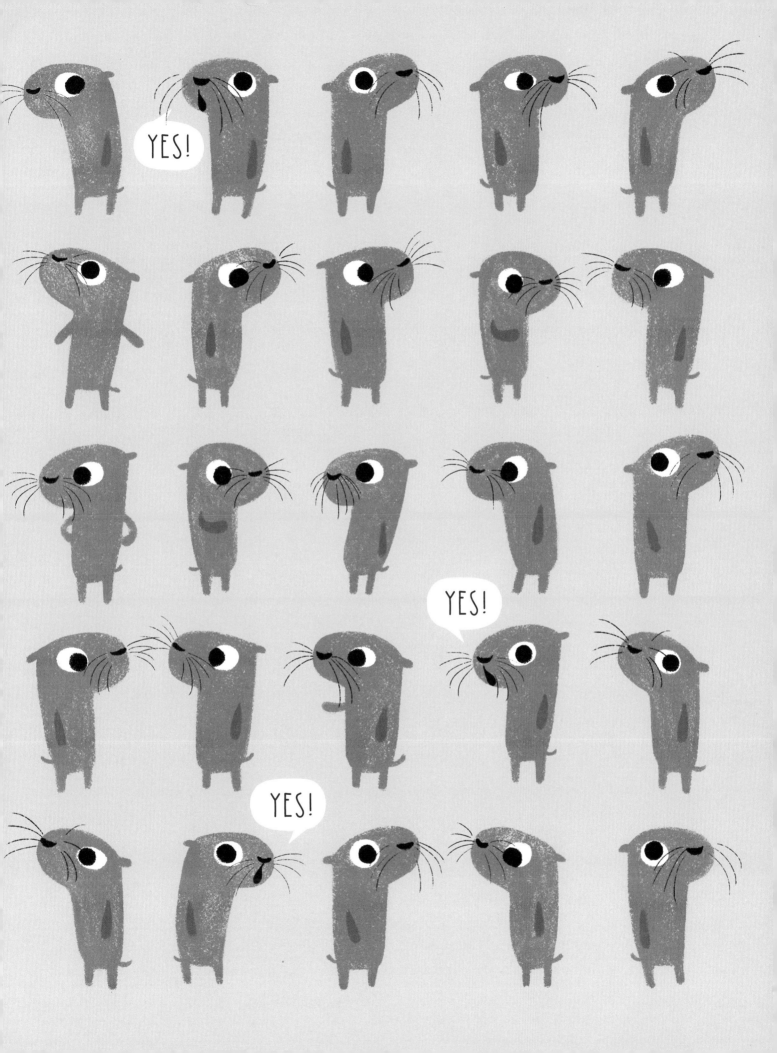

JOHN BRIGGS is a longtime reporter and editor who once spent three years as a children's TV critic. Yes, he was actually paid to watch children's television (which he thought needed more lemmings). Today, he happily writes books for children. A native of Philadelphia, John currently lives in upstate New York, where he has never, ever jumped off a cliff.

NICOLA SLATER is a professional illustrator and a semi-professional coffee-drinker. She studied illustration at Buckinghamshire Chilterns University and now lives and works among utter chaos in Manchester with her family and a very bad cat, which she is planning to trade in for a lemming.